Queen Ella's Feet

Level 3B

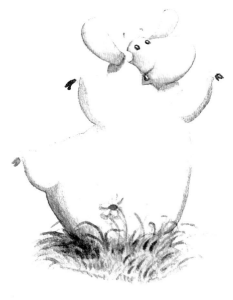

Written by Sally Grindley
Illustrated by Sandra Aguilar

What is synthetic phonics?

Synthetic phonics teaches children to recognise the sounds of letters and to blend 'synthesise' them together to make whole words.

Understanding sound/letter relationships gives children the confidence and ability to read unfamiliar words, without having to rely on memory or guesswork; this helps them progress towards independent reading.

Did you know? Spoken English uses more than 40 speech sounds. Each sound is called a *phoneme*. Some phonemes relate to a single letter (d-o-g) and others to combinations of letters (sh-ar-p). When a phoneme is written down it is called a *grapheme*. Teaching these sounds, matching them to their written form and sounding out words for reading is the basis of synthetic phonics.

Consultant

I love reading phonics has been created in consultation with language expert Abigail Steel. She has a background in teaching and teacher training and is a respected expert in the field of Synthetic Phonics. Abigail Steel is a regular contributor to educational publications. Her international education consultancy supports parents and teachers in the promotion of literacy skills.

Reading tips

This book focuses on the ee sound as in feet.

Tricky words in this book

Any words in bold may have unusual spellings or are new and have not yet been introduced.

Tricky words in this book:

my cold I to for her
you said the cart by

Extra ways to have fun with this book

After the reader has finished the story, ask them questions about what they have just read:

Why is the Queen unhappy at the beginning of the story?
Why does the maid look for a sheep?

Explain that the two letters 'ee' make one sound. Think of other words that use the 'ee' sound, such as *sheep* and *feet*.

I eat grass
in the day and
I read books
at night.

A pronunciation guide

This grid highlights the sounds used in the story and offers a guide on how to say them.

s	a	t	p	i
as in sat	as in ant	as in tin	as in pig	as in ink
n	c	e	h	r
as in net	as in cat	as in egg	as in hen	as in rat
m	d	g	o	u
as in mug	as in dog	as in get	as in ox	as in up
l	f	b	j	v
as in log	as in fan	as in bag	as in jug	as in van
w	z	y	k	qu
as in wet	as in zip	as in yet	as in kit	as in quick
x	ff	ll	ss	zz
as in box	as in off	as in ball	as in kiss	as in buzz
ck	pp	nn	rr	gg
as in duck	as in puppy	as in bunny	as in arrow	as in egg
dd	bb	tt	sh	ch
as in daddy	as in chubby	as in attic	as in shop	as in chip
th	th	ng	nk	le
as in them	as in the	as in sing	as in sunk	as in bottle
ai	ee			
as in rain	as in feet			

Be careful not to add an 'uh' sound to 's', 't', 'p', 'c', 'h', 'r', 'm', 'd', 'g', 'l', 'f' and 'b'. For example, say 'fff' not 'fuh' and 'sss' not 'suh'.

'**My** feet feel **cold**,' weeps Queen Ella. '**I** need **to** keep my feet hot.'

'Queen Ella needs a big sheet **for her** feet!' **said** King Alex.

'I will seek a sheep,'
said Jen **the** maid.

Jen gets in a **cart**.

'I need a sheep,' Jen said to a bee.

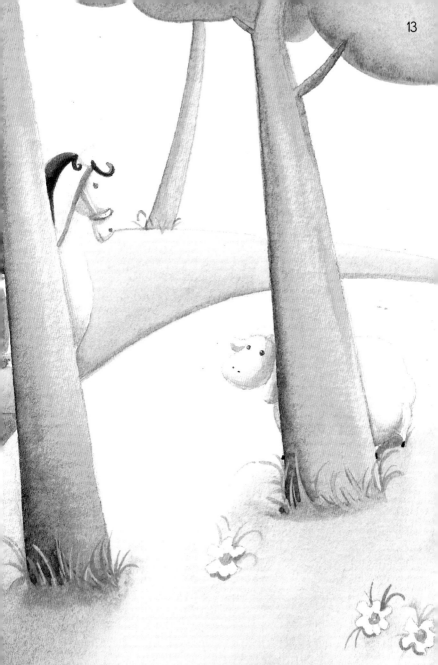

'A sheep?' said the bee.
'I see a sheep **by** that tree.'

'Queen Ella needs a sheep,'
said the bee to the sheep.

'Will I meet Queen Ella?'
said the sheep.

'**You** will meet Queen Ella,' said Jen.

'Queen Ella needs a sheep
for her feet.'

The sheep got in the cart.

'A sheep for Queen Ella's feet,'
said Jen to King Alex.

'A sheep?' said King Alex.
'But Queen Ella needs
a sheet not a sheep!'

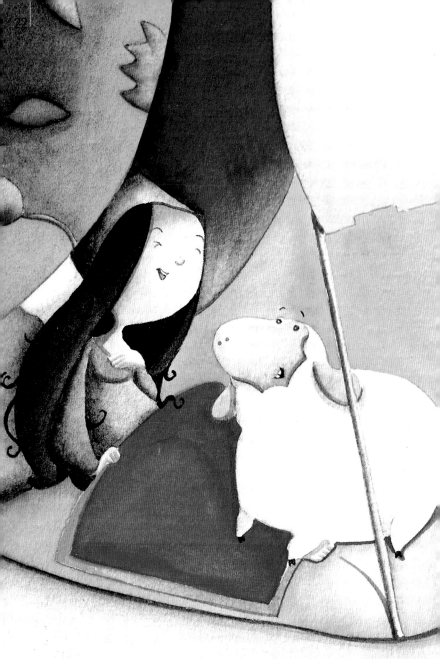

'I will keep the sheep for my feet!'
said Queen Ella.

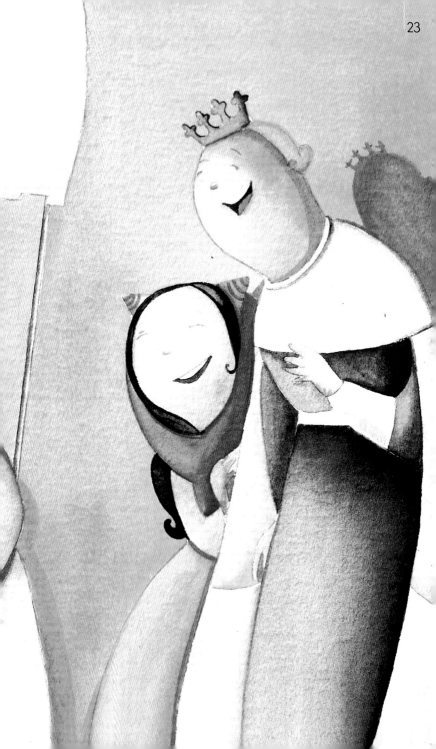

OVER 48 TITLES IN SIX LEVELS
Abigail Steel recommends...

Some titles from Level 1

Bad Rat
978-1-84898-277-2

The Best Gift
978-1-84898-396-0

Clint and Grant Play I-Spy
978-1-84898-548-3

Gran and Bret's Trip
978-1-84898-547-6

Some titles from Level 2

Wish Fish
978-1-84898-386-1

Chuck and Duck
978-1-84898-387-8

Pink Bunny
978-1-84898-550-6

Let's go to the Swings
978-1-84898-549-0

Other titles to enjoy from Level 3

Bart's Go-Cart
978-1-84898-552-0

The Pop Duet
978-1-84898-551-3

Puff Flies
978-1-84898-399-1

An Hachette UK Company
www.hachette.co.uk

Copyright © Octopus Publishing Group Ltd 2012
First published in Great Britain in 2012 by TickTock, an imprint of Octopus Publishing Group Ltd,
Endeavour House, 189 Shaftesbury Avenue, London WC2H 8JY.
www.octopusbooks.co.uk

ISBN 978 1 84898 398 4

Printed and bound in China
10 9 8 7 6 5 4 3 2